A Labor Day Hooray

Written and Illustrated by Dee Smith

Copyright © 2016

Today, mom and dad are home to stay.

They are off from work.

It's Labor Day!

It's on the first Monday of every September.

It's a day for workers to relax.

This day is fun to remember.

There are all kinds of jobs that we celebrate!

We appreciate them all on this special date.

The bakers.

The teachers.

The construction workers too.

We all cherish the forms of work they do.

Each worker contributes in a special way.

They may inform us.

They may construct where we live or play.

They may help us learn.

They may help things grow.

They may heal us.

They may even put on a show.

They may prepare crops for us to buy and eat.

They may drive our busses after we take a seat.

They may be the ones there to protect us all.

They might put out fires in buildings, big and small.

No matter the job one thing remains true.

Labor Day is a celebration of the amazing things they do.

Happy Labor Day Everyone!

Thank You!

Thank you so much for reading this book.
It means the world to me!
If you liked the book I would much appreciate if you would write a Review on Amazon. I am so thankful for each and every person supporting my dream of being a writer for children. Because you have read this book, yes that means YOU too! Thanks Again!
Stay tuned for more titles on my website Deesignery.com

Regards,
Dee

About the Author:

My name is Dee Smith. I am an Author and Illustrator. My hobbies include graphic design, puppetry, balloon twisting, drawing and of course writing. I am dedicated to my mission of keeping children entertained in fun and innovative ways.

Made in the USA
Las Vegas, NV
27 August 2021